Some Smug Slug

by Pamela Duncan Edwards
illustrated by Henry Cole

HarperCollins*Publishers*

The illustrations in this book were painted with acrylic paints and
colored pencils on Arches Hot Press watercolor paper.

S
O
M
E
S
M
U
G
S
L
U
G

Text copyright © 1996 by Pamela Duncan Edwards
Illustrations copyright © 1996 by Henry Cole
Printed in the U.S.A. All rights reserved.

Library of Congress Cataloging-in-Publication Data
Edwards, Pamela.
   Some smug slug / by Pamela Duncan Edwards ; illustrated by Henry
Cole.
       p.   cm.
   Summary: A smug slug that will not listen to the animals around it
comes to an unexpected end.
   ISBN 0-06-024789-4. — ISBN 0-06-024792-4 (lib. bdg.)
   [1. Slugs (Mollusks)—Fiction.   2. Animals—Fiction.]   I. Cole, Henry,
ill.   II. Title.
PZ7.E26365So   1996   94-18682
[E]—dc20   CIP
                                                                          AC

Typography by Elynn Cohen
1   2   3   4   5   6   7   8   9   10
❖
First Edition

For dear Peter,
who would have laughed.
—P.D.E.

Stephen—Scooby!
—H.C.

One summer Sunday
while strolling on soil,

4

with its antennae signaling,
a slug sensed a slope.

Slowly the slug started
up the steep surface,
stringing behind it
scribble sparkling like silk.

"Stop!" screamed a sparrow,
shattering the silence.

"Save him!" shrieked a spider,
scurrying down its strand.

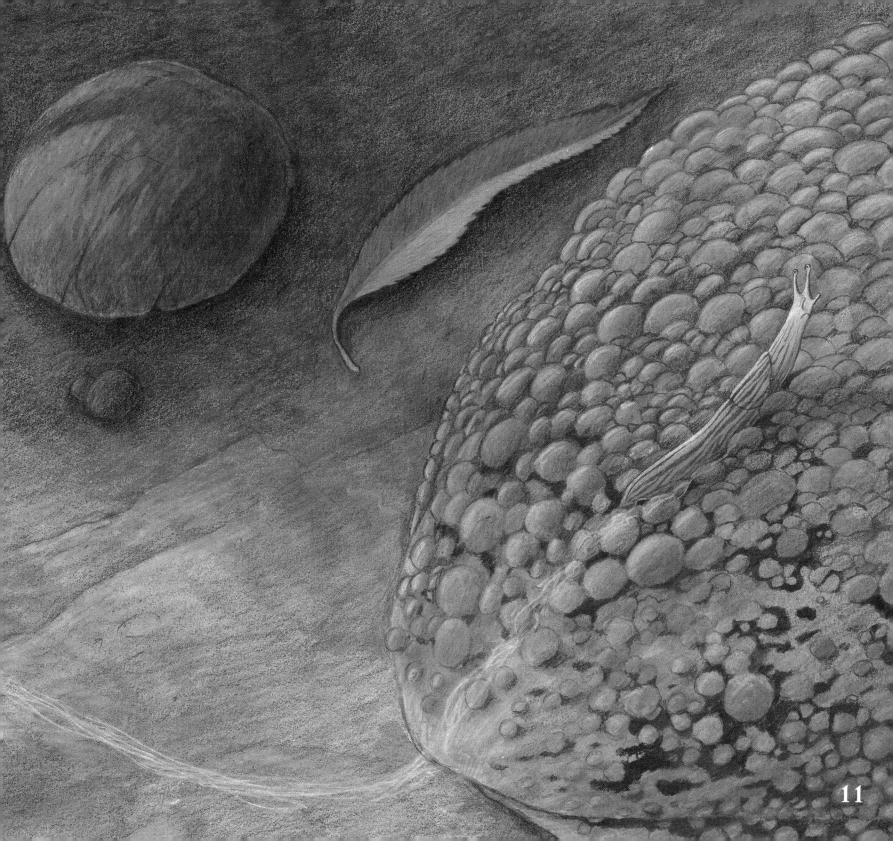

11

"Silly," sighed a swallowtail,
swooshing through the spice bush.

13

"Saphead!" snickered a skink
as its sapphire tail swished.

With a shrug of its shoulders, on the slug sauntered. With a swagger it slithered up, up the slant.

"Show-off," scolded a squirrel,
storing nuts for the season.

"So sad," squealed a stink bug, shivering on a stem.

17

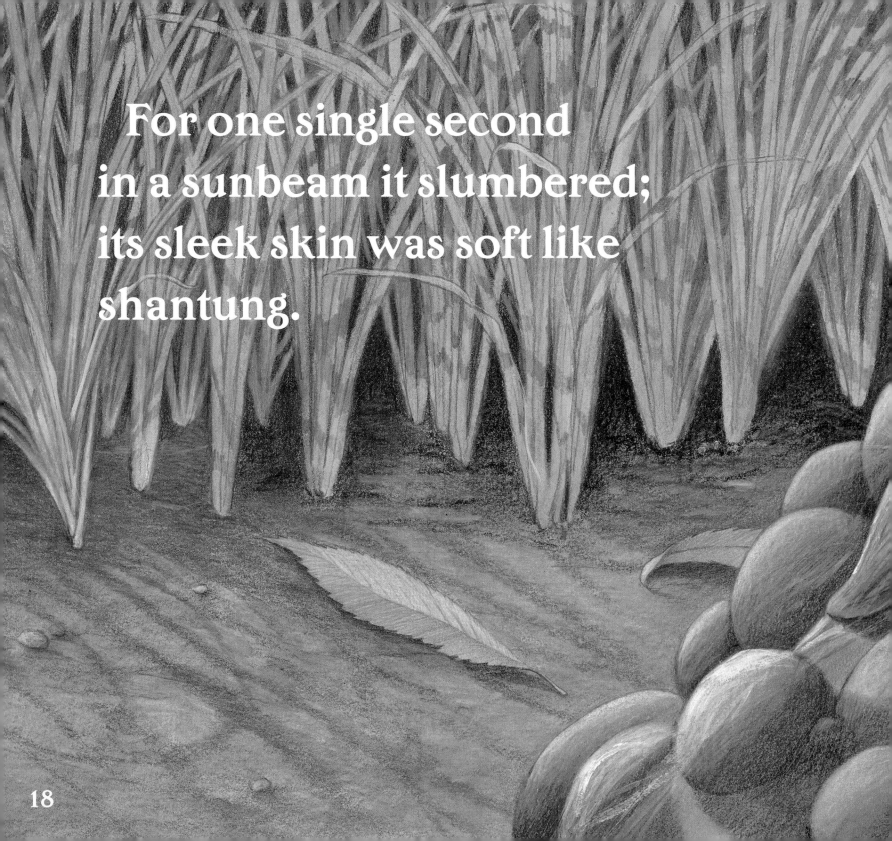

For one single second
in a sunbeam it slumbered;
its sleek skin was soft like
shantung.

19

Seldom swerving or straggling
or swaying or skewing,

the smug slug shambled on.

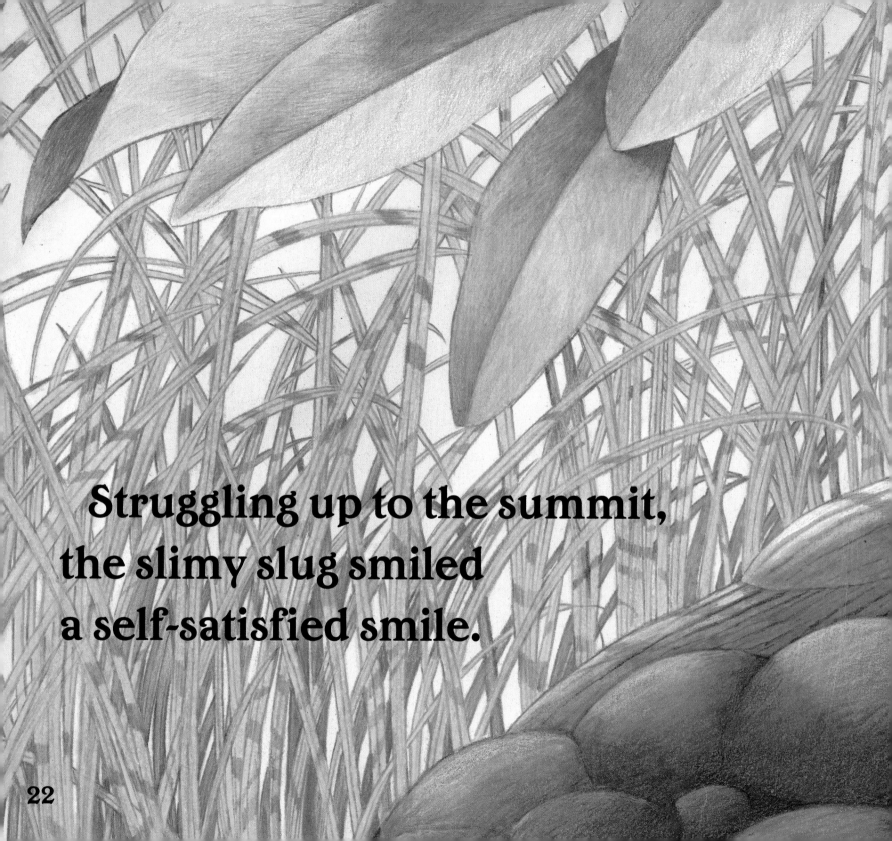

Struggling up to the summit,
the slimy slug smiled
a self-satisfied smile.

In spite of sinister signs,
it showed no suspicion,

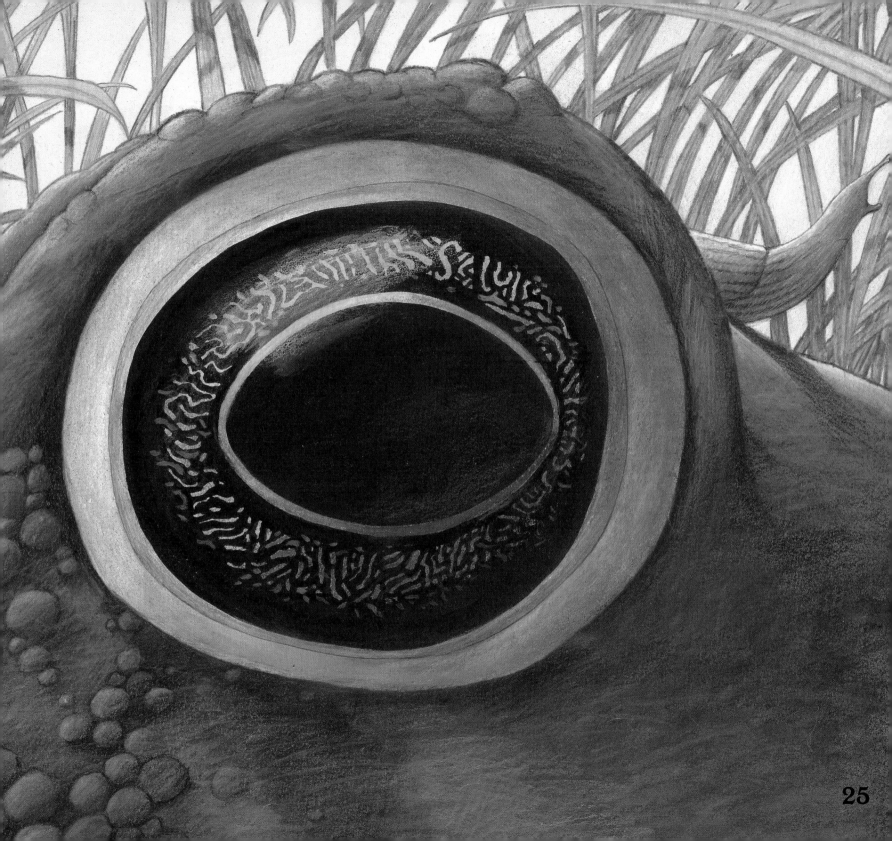

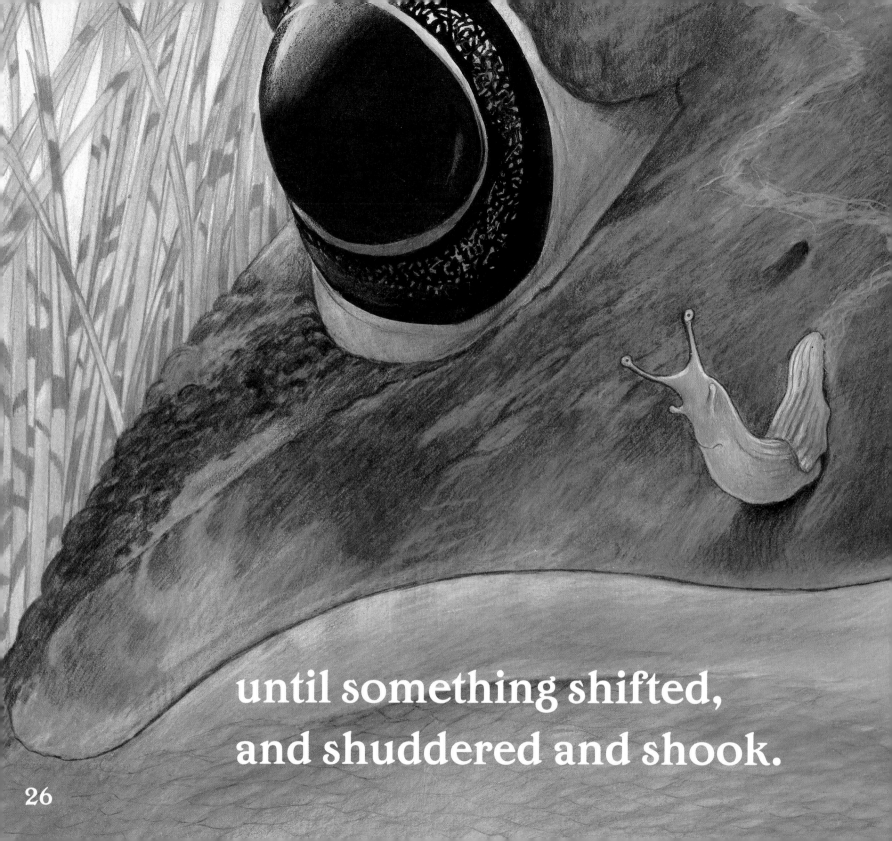

until something shifted,
and shuddered and shook.

That sly, slippery slope
was simply a sham.

Such a shock, such a shame.

29

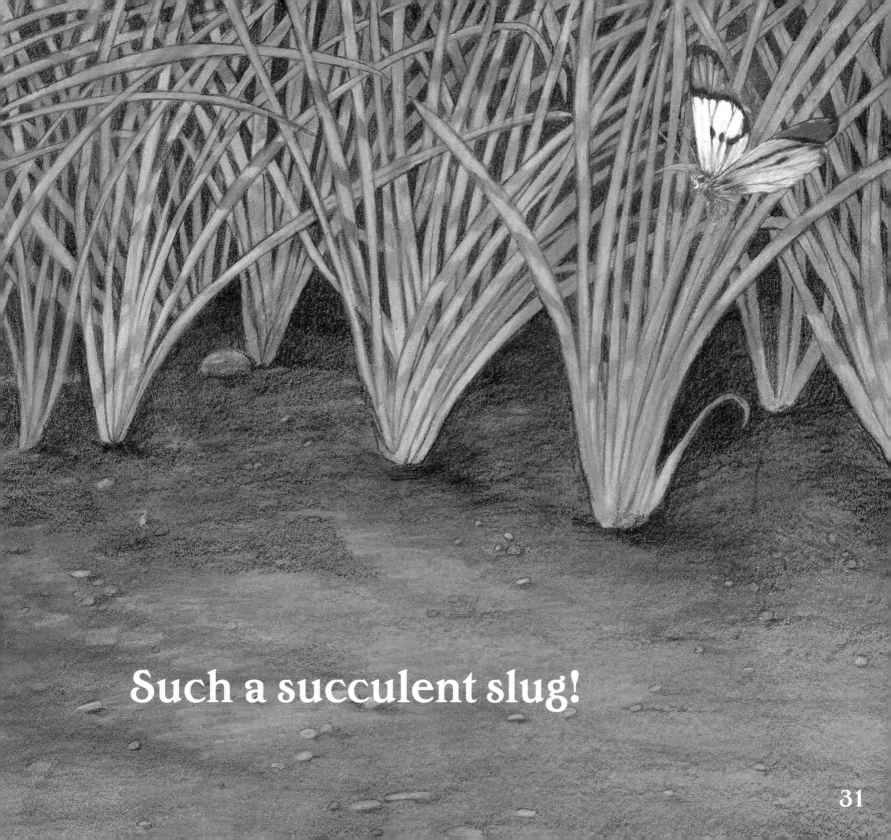

Such a succulent slug!

31

Somewhere in this story,
did you see a skunk, a snake, a salamander,
and two snails spying on the slug?

Also hidden in each picture is an "S" shape.
Can you spot it?